On the Run

Anne Roberts

DEDICATIONS

I DEDICATE THIS SHORT STORY TO MY LATE
HUSBAND MIKE. WRITING WAS HIS THING AND
HE WILL BE PLEASED I'VE DONE SOMETHING
WITH MY SCRIBBLES .

CONTENTS

ACKNOWLEDGMENTS

I HAVE TO THANK ALL THE PEOPLE WHO BELIEVED ME THIS LAST DECADE OR MORE ABOUT THE EXISTENCE OF THIS ESCAPEE , TO PAUL GASH WHO INITIALLY ALERTED ME TO IT BEING ON OUR LAND AS HE WATCHED IT FROM HIS TRACTOR , NIGEL ANOTHER NEIGHBOUR AND GOOD FRIEND WHO HAS SEEN IT A FEW TIMES , ENOUGH FOR ME TO KNOW I WASN'T GOING MAD. MY MOTHER MARY WHO WAS WITH ME ON A COUPLE OF OCCASIONS WHEN WE SAW IT AND MY FATHER SELWYN AND SISTER LINDA WHO IN FACT CAME TO MY RESCUE WITH COAL SHOVELS AND BATS WHEN I HAD A CLOSE ENCOUNTER ON THE YARD AND LOCKED MYSELF AWAY IN A SHED .LASTLY A HUGE THANK YOU TO HAYLEY MITCHELL MY STEP GRANDDAUGHTER FOR HELPING ME THROUGH ALL THE TECHY SIDE OF THINGS AND FOR PROOF READING AND FORMATTING MY SCRIBBLES INTO SOMETHING LEGIBLE .

FREEDOM

Arial view of Ben's territory

Ben lay down in the long grass.   From this height he could look down towards the sea and see the farmland stretching towards the saltings and the shore. Since his escape three years before life had been an increasing struggle but days like this seemed to make it worthwhile.

There were people working on the land below; he saw them often and had got used to them being around.   Sometimes he was only metres away from them and they did not know he was there. He had got very good at hiding. He had to!

He could not cope with his imprisonment; he loved the outdoors too much for that, but he had been careless and he had been caught. He had no intention of being caught again. For months after his escape small parties of men had been searching for him and it had been hard surviving- he had chosen the wrong time of year for his escape and food was scarce. There was plenty about but catching it was a problem and many a day he had gone hungry until the pain gnawing at his insides was almost unbearable.

Ben knew the area quite well by now and had stayed in the vicinity throughout the time since his escape. He moved about mostly at night and very early morning and realised that the best time to find himself a meal was just as the sun was rising.

He stretched and yawned comfortably in the sunshine; satisfied and full from a meal of pheasant. It was a little easier to see the rabbits and wildfowl at the moment as the people he saw down below were using machinery to cut the grass. The only problem with this was that he could see his meals walking around a lot more clearly, but they could also see him and something of his size had difficulty moving without being seen.

There were three people below. If they looked up in the right place, they probably could have seen him, but he had at least learnt to keep in the shadows of the rocky outcrops and remain unseen. It was a good feeling to see life go on and knowing people were oblivious to him being there. They were moving the horses again, at this time of year they moved quite often from field to field and then the fields would be worked with machinery for a few days. Then because of the lay of the land the fields would be empty and silent for a few weeks. At these times he could risk moving down the hillside and try to catch a few rabbits but had to be careful not to leave any trace of himself. He had done this twice and nearly been caught, so he knew to be careful.

Ben was not keen on the horses and it seemed they did not like him very much either. When he had been very hungry and walked through them to get to the lower ground to get to the saltings they started to stampede around him and strike at him with their feet and he caught a few blows on his back and head. He could smell the fear on them as he made his way down the field.

His home now consisted of two caves where, by and large, he was left in peace. They were old mine workings which actually linked together under the hill. This year for the first time since he found them, he was able to get right through the system as it had been so dry the water table had lowered and the normally full caves were dry. This had enabled him to increase his territory a little without being seen.

The hillside he lived on was very quiet; occasionally someone would make his or her way through the overgrown wilderness to walk the path but that was very rare. There were a couple of hundred acres of land which was just gorse, bracken, blackthorn and woodland that no one ever went into. Ideal for an escapee. He had learnt to his peril the danger of blackthorn when he had a spike in his foot which had caused him intense pain for weeks and made him feel quite ill.

His cave was not far off a path but people did not bother with it. The occasional dog sniffed about but always seemed wary of going further than the mouth. Both caves were entered downwards via a hole in the ground and were not very inviting, anyway he managed to keep reasonably warm and dry in there. He had dragged in a lot of bracken early on and these provided him with a comfortable, if not itchy, bed as they had dried.

SUMMER LIVING

On days like this the beach became very busy. There were people everywhere, paddling, swimming and flying kites. Once or twice he had quietly crept down to a rough area near the car park; he could smell food but knew instinctively it was too risky to chance going any nearer. It was difficult moving through the undergrowth as he was tugged at by sharp brambles and blackthorn bushes and the bracken was almost too high to see over. He relied largely on his acute sense of smell and hearing to know how close he was to the seashore and the people.

No one expected to see him there as most of the people here changed daily. It was so busy the locals kept away or just got on with their work and most of those had not heard of his escape at the time so no one was actively looking for him. In any case none of the locals would believe there was an escapee on the run in this quiet neck of the woods.

Hay making on the lower slopes

It would not be long until he was hungry again. Most of his time these days was taken up with looking for food or at least thinking about food. The only thing he did miss about his imprisonment was that he was, at least, given a square meal daily and in fact had become a bit fat and lazy due to lack of exercise. It is not easy to do a lot in a twelve by twelve area. Things were getting quieter down below now. The horses were settling down after moving fields, cars were leaving the beach; soon it would be quiet although there would be a few local regulars out walking after the visitors had left. Someone was working by a gateway down below; putting in new gateposts by the look of things, another person was nearby lifting a gate off a trailer, their voices carried towards him on the breeze coming off the sea. He wasn't worried as he stretched and yawned and waited for nightfall so he could go and find some food.

Dusk came and the area gradually became empty of people. The sky over the bay became red and orange as the sun got lower; the sea took on the same light, so that it was difficult to tell where the sky stopped and the sea started. The warm breeze just about kept him cool after the heat of the day. He didn't particularly enjoy being too hot and was happy to stay in the shadows of the crags on the hill watching life pass by- if only people knew how close he was to them all the time.

Birds could be heard coming in to roost and he could still make out the odd rabbit scampering along below; it was more difficult for them to hide now that the fields had been mown. In fact, he often watched the fox family who lived just above the salting's play in the longer grass at the edges of the fields which had been too steep to mow. They used to live higher up the hill, but probably had become aware of his presence and kept their distance.

The only problem with foxes was that often at night men with big lamps would come out looking for them. He had once come almost face to face with some of these men; he had wandered at night away from his usual nocturnal territory to hunt and suddenly was confronted by a blinding light. Immediately he crouched and turned away and made his swift escape through the undergrowth. This was the time he had stood on a broken blackthorn branch which had penetrated into his foot. He had let out a yowl but had to keep running for fear of being caught. To his surprise no one seemed to follow him but as he limped his way back to the nearest cave entrance, that night he went hungry. He had a sore foot for quite a while after that night and had felt tired and ill for days. He kept low, and stayed in the cave.

CONFRONTATIONS

Night had fallen slowly; lights had come on in the houses and small farms around him and he felt safe enveloped in the darkness. A strong smell of mown grass filled the air and dulled his senses slightly to any other scents in the air. He could safely make his way now from his viewpoint and descend into the wetlands below.

 The horses had moved so he crossed the field undisturbed. They were, however, aware of his movements and a couple lifted their heads as he passed their gate; they snorted and high tailed it towards the others – he hated horses! He had to pass a cottage to enter the woods; he paused and listened, quiet chatter, then a dog barked. He tried to keep himself clean but he thought they could probably smell him when he was near.

He often watched them in the daytime, nose down following the track he had taken during the night, usually followed by a lot of shouting of "Come here dog" as the dog disappeared further from the owner's sight. He had come across a couple of dogs but when they got closer to him, they backed off and ran barking back to their owners.

The wood was very dark by now- a glimmer of summer night sky occasionally seen through a gap in the canopy; the smell of wild garlic was fading now as the summer wore on. He found it quite pungent and sickly earlier on in the summer. No one had ever come to this place at night and it reinforced his feeling of security. At the other end of the wood there was a stream where he often drank with a house right next to it, but most of the time it was empty.

Down the road from this house was a farm yard; he was wary of this place as there were a couple of dogs that made a noise if he came too close. He had learnt since that they were shut in at night sometimes giving him a chance to check the dustbins for any tasty morsels. From here he could carry on across the darkened fields without touching a road and go to places where he had been lucky on previous occasions and caught a rabbit.

His night time wanderings often took him miles from his cave home, but he knew the area well now and the necessity to find his food meant that he had built up quite a degree of fitness which he had not possessed before. He always made his way back by the time the sun was starting to rise behind the hill. Once he had been caught in a car's headlight as he had taken a chance and crossed a road, he managed to jump onto and over a wall and stayed close to it as he went as fast as he could towards familiar ground. The car had stopped, he heard voices and saw the light of a torch in the distance before he heard doors bang and the car drive off. He often wondered if people had imagined seeing him and brushed it off as a trick of the half-light.

When he got back to the cave, he checked around the entrance in case he had any unwanted visitors while he was away. Satisfied it was empty he went in. He never brought any food he caught back here for fear of attracting attention by dogs and in turn their owners.

The cave was cool even in this weather. The mouth of the tunnel was narrow and quite a squeeze for a short distance then it opened up into a larger cavern where he got fresh water to drink. A small tunnel came from the side at this point and disappeared as a hole in the ground. Along it ran a clear stream of water. Sometimes in winter it was difficult to get past this point when the water levels outside were high as well and he had to use another entrance then.

From this larger area the tunnel went eastwards under the hill and had larger caverns along its end. At one point there was an open hole to the sky above which allowed in some welcome fresh air. Beyond this point the cave split into two. He slept at the dead end in the right-hand fork. It was not the most pleasant-smelling place now, but he was undisturbed and knew he could sleep away the daylight hours if he so wanted. The left-hand fork continued in a series of tunnels and caverns until it came out nearer the Church by the other end of the beach. He had to be careful making an exit here as it was, in fact, quite close to a house and the owners were keen gardeners who spent most of their time outdoors.

He had come across their cat one day which in its fright at suddenly meeting him at the mouth of the tunnel had given him a nasty scratch across the face. He thought he had hurt the cat in the confrontation as although he was obviously far bigger it had attacked him with some ferocity and he took a couple of swipes at it as it went for his face.
He did not see the cat there again.

He made himself comfortable in what was now very much his home. At times like this he wished very much that he had a companion to share day to day things with but it couldn't be. He fell asleep, one ear half listening to the sound of the crows drifting down through the sky hole. His body seemed trained to be aware of any new noise that may be heard.

Earlier in the year what turned out to be a local university potholing club had appeared in the wood and he had to make a hasty exit to high ground for a few hours. Luckily, he never left any evidence of his residency in the cave.

SILLY RISKS

Summer wore on into autumn and his immediate area became generally quieter; there were fewer people on the beach apart from a couple of times a week when people appeared with their various dogs. He needed to be very careful during these days to keep away from the lower beach areas as quite a few dogs had picked up on his scent where he had walked through the undergrowth to get into the woodland and had followed him much to the distress of the owners who could be heard below shouting and calling their disobedient canines. The smaller the dog, funnily enough, the more likely they were to stand their ground. These needed a good backhander before they went yelping back to their concerned owners. He had never really left his mark on any of them but was tempted more than once.

As the autumn moved into winter, he got a little careless in his movements. The small mammals he managed to survive on got more difficult to find. The undergrowth was dying away rapidly and they had less cover but likewise so did he; he became easier to see therefore the creatures had long gone before he could catch them.

One day, however, he got far too careless in his quest to satisfy his hunger. It was three days since he had eaten a square meal and had ventured onto the lane which led to the beach. A rabbit was browsing on the remaining juicy stems hidden under the gorse bushes at the edge of the field seemingly oblivious to him being close. He lay low to the ground stretched almost across the width of the narrow road and waited his chance to pounce when he heard the sound of approaching hoof beats. A quick look confirmed two horses coming in his direction. A few more seconds was all he wanted; he almost held his breath waiting for the right moment when suddenly he heard voices and horror of horror two people were with the horses. He had not noticed them at first as the horses were skittish and partly curled around the handlers. There was a car coming too - time for a sharp exit he thought and set off up the lane away from them, he hurriedly looked for a gap in the right-hand bank to make his escape but even as he reached the top of the bank the people had reached the gap and were watching him sprint away.

That had been a really stupid chance to take; he had to be careful not to repeat his foolishness. People who had known originally about his escape would have long left the area but rumours got around and he had an inkling that more people were aware of his being there though no one seemed to be making a concerted effort to find him. If he was to survive out here, he had to be doubly careful.

The herd that caused him trouble

MISERY

Winter came wetly, the dampness seeping determinedly into his very pores, chilling him to the core; it was miserable for him in the cave, the water levels had risen and the sogginess was all-pervading. He went very hungry at this time. All the animals were doing exactly as he was - keeping their heads down and trying miserably to stay warm.

There was activity again on the fields. People came on a regular basis to fill the big round metal rings with hay for the horses – the horses he had upset more than once when they were busy eating by using the cover of darkness and undergrowth to get closer to the dune areas near the sea. He had often sent the horses scurrying and snorting away from their food supply.

The dune area often provided him with a much-appreciated meal when the odd rabbit dared leave its burrow in search of sustenance. One evening he had almost been cornered in a nearby garden. He sat in the shadows and watched as a family enjoyed a meal together, the children giggling happily, and most certainly he savoured the smell of the meal.

He had lain under the hedge for a couple of hours listening and dozing before making his way back to the cave. He enjoyed visiting that particular garden; he had indeed managed to take a couple of chickens in the past and no doubt the local foxes had been blamed. More than once he had been tempted by the goats kept at the house but they were always too alert to his presence.

During the previous winter the property had been empty for quite a long time apart from the goats being there; he had often enjoyed the quiet and lain peacefully observing his surroundings during the early afternoons but as the summer had worn on the family had returned. In fact, he had been seen by one of the family one day as he crossed the field. There had been lots of activity then and he had needed to keep very quiet for a seemingly long time that day as men walked the fields searching for him. There was also a helicopter in the sky hovering like a bird of prey above him. Some men had actually walked within five feet of him at one point only the thick brambles hiding him as they walked past. There was lots of shouting and general excitement for a long time.

There was noise well into the night when the interest in him was resurrected for what seemed a very long time. His life became very difficult. He returned to his cave and kept quiet for what seemed like weeks.

HUNGER

Hunger pangs overtook his sensibility as winter became colder; the rain relented a little and a long period of frost and snow took over. Not only was finding food difficult at this time so was quenching his thirst. A thick layer of ice covered most of his usual waterholes and sometimes he was driven down to the marsh to drink out of the river inlet except when the tide drove the streams landwards and with it the salt water. He hated the taste of that. He had come across some people a few times during mid winter but as many people did not believe that such an escapee could be present in the area, they almost disregarded the sightings and got on with their lives.

One evening he thought his birthday had come. The horses nearby had become very fractious and uneasy and the reason became very clear to see. A mare had foaled, unexpectedly and early by the looks of the foal on the ground. He had come across the horses earlier in the evening when he came out of his woodland shelter; they had taken off in fright and had taken a long time to settle again. He quietly crept closer to the small animal on the floor. He could not detect any movement and closer and closer he got - getting excited now at the thought of an opportune meal.

Suddenly a scuffle behind him took his attention; a great white horse appeared at his right shoulder, it rose above him and struck out at him with a ferocity that caught him totally off balance and caused him to roll onto his back. Thud. Again, he was struck this time in the softness of his belly. It took the wind right out of him and rendered him immobile for what seemed like minutes. The horses stood off; he could smell the fear and hate emanating from them.

The white horse moved forwards again. He leapt at the small mound on the ground; it was still wet. He tried to grab it, it slipped from his grip, and the white horse lunged at him again - this time he had to protect himself. He leapt up, dodging the flying hooves, lunged for the horses back and clung on while it bucked and plunged under him.

All the others ran with it. He loosened his grasp and knowing he would not be able to bring it down ran back to the tiny corpse, grabbed it and made his way down the sloped field. He got as far as the hedge and dropped his prey. He laid breathlessly listening to the distant horses now, the odd high pitch snort audible above the wind off the sea. In time over the next few hours he fed on the trophy till he had his fill. He crept off to his cave as dawn was breaking, the horses had still not returned.

Mike, the author's husband, checking the stock

The next day he went to the rocky crags above the little farm enjoying a feeling of fullness he had not felt for what seemed like weeks, in fact he did not really feel inclined to do much at all that day. Below him people walked the fields going their separate ways along the hedgerows until one of them came across the remains of the foal. He had only left a hind leg - even he had a limit to his appetite. He could see the white horse which had attacked him being led away towards the gate. He was surprised not to be feeling sorer after his beating but he supposed he was so toned and hard now from all the exercise that his body deflected the blows almost by instinct.

For days after this incident there were people around at all hours of the night; he supposed, looking for him. He had to lay low. Luckily his last feast would sustain him for a couple of days.

Things quietened down but the weather remained cold, snowfall making it difficult for him to move around unseen. He had to stay under cover of the woodland surrounding the cave system. In fact, the cave system was the easiest way to move around; both the ends he used were well hidden. Only once had he been startled by two horses who had rushed through a gateway and almost trampled him. This was one of the very few times he had shouted out in self-defence. A person had quickly followed the horses but he had made his way over the hedge before she got there or rather scrambled through the hedge just in time.

Each time he had been seen or nearly seen interest in him seemed to reignite for a few days and then quickly die down again.

A couple of times in the last two years people who seemed to be aware of his being in the area made a concerted effort to track him. They looked for footprints, remains of his meals, and even looked at areas where he had relieved himself, but he was quite an expert at hiding by now, the only time he was seen now was at night when the odd late car caught him out when crossing a road was necessary.

PAST TIMES

When he had escaped it had been a quiet affair; more than likely because the powers that be did not want to declare his escape to the general public. He could be dangerous although he had never had need to be. He did not like his captivity certainly from the fact that he had no real freedom to move around and his prison was a little small for his needs. But he was well looked after, most of his needs were met – well maybe apart from the company of the opposite sex, but then what he had never had he shouldn't ever miss. His food had been appetizing and he never recalled feeling hungry. Recently though more than once he had felt this urge for company which had caused him to call out at night.

Yes times were hard now, being self-sufficient, but he was comforted in the fact that he had a huge area which was poorly populated and allowed him great freedom albeit in the hours of darkness. Maybe one day his luck would turn and the girl of his dreams would appear from somewhere. In his long hours of solitude he often thought that maybe recapture would make his life a lot more comfortable but his innate instinct to maintain his freedom overtook any feelings that he ever got of giving himself up.

That however was about to change; he was almost to lose his freedom and if he was not careful - his life.

CLOSE CALL

He laid lazily in his favourite tree branch.   It was a place he liked to be because he could watch the world go by and he was quite sure no one could see him because of the way the tree branches spread out around him; it was a little more exposed and windy in the winter without the greenery around him but he could not be seen from the road. Only someone actually walking in the field and actively looking up for him would be able to see him and to date no one had gone to the effort of doing that.

The fields where this tree stood was fairly near to the beach but he could get to it quite easily by crossing the lane when it was quiet and then entering the field and crossing directly into a little wooded copse which was very swampy in the winter. A well-worn path trampled by the horses made it a quick and easy route for him to get to his tree. He wasn't very high up - around fifteen feet or so - but it was an easy climb for his now agile and strong body.

The other big advantage here was his elevated view of the goings on below and the easy jump down to catch any unsuspecting rabbits feeding below.   He was onto them and back in the tree almost before their mates had noticed they had gone.

The weather was fair; in fact, it had been dry but cold for a week or so. He could cope with that, his coat was thick, it was the relentless rain that got right through to his bones and took him days to dry.
He dozed and yawned. The horses who lived in that field were at the other end happily munching away at a newly delivered big bale. The

person who bought the hay came around three days a week and checked the horses each time. She had been quite close to the tree where he lay often but he remained silent, almost not breathing for fear of being heard. He felt she was aware of the possibility of seeing him but also felt she was not purposely seeking him out.

She had returned this day, however, with two men. They walked directly towards the tree where he lay, they talked animatedly and were looking very closely at the trees on the way to where he was. They seemed to be examining the tree trunks and the immediate area surrounding the tree. One man was taking pictures of whatever the other man was pointing at. They seemed to be getting very excited about something they had found. It was only because of this find that they did not come any closer to where he was. He was literally ten feet away from them and convinced himself that they would smell him if he wasn't careful.

After what seemed like an age they moved on a bit to another group of trees and brambles and spent a while in there pushing their way into the dense undergrowth. He did not go that way often himself as it caught and snagged the skin on his legs and made movement very difficult. It dawned on him at that point that they could be actively looking for evidence of him having been there. He was shocked at this realisation and all sensibility left him at this point, so did any sense of self-preservation which he had prided himself on since his initial escape.

Then he made his first mistake – he leapt down out of the tree. The horses who were still eating suddenly scuttled away and snorted; he made for the swamp and the copse aiming to get to higher ground. A shout was heard behind him- the woman had seen him, the men then joined in the shouting and the taller of the two started sprinting clumsily after him. The ground was very soggy so his movement in heavy wellingtons was difficult. The other two people joined in the run; the woman caught up with the man quite quickly whereas the second man made for the gate where they had left a vehicle.
Ben broke out of the cover of the spindly trees, covered the rest of the field in what seemed like three giant leaps, got under the fence, over the road into the next field and then proceeded to sprint

effortlessly over the now drier terrain as he followed the track to the higher ground. He didn't pause until he reached the woodland at the base of the rock outcrops on the hill. He stopped and listened but could not make out any sounds of the three people following him. He climbed further through the dead heather and brown wilted bracken hiding his presence in the shadow of the rocks. He was panting now, his breath coming in short gasps but he had got away. From his vantage point he turned when he heard a car departing from the bottom… they were going.

LYING LOW

He stayed up on the hill for the next few days. It had unnerved him but on the other hand he had maybe got a little complacent and not as careful, perhaps because he was at last feeling comfortable in his environment which he now looked upon as being his territory. It was certainly no one else's; he was the only one living like this.

He caught a pheasant on the second day after the chase - stalked it and caught it almost as if he was on automatic pilot. It was instinct taking over because when he had got round to it, he wasn't even hungry.

Life had got a little more difficult since he had been seen. The same men had returned to the lower fields; they wandered in and out of the undergrowth and seemed to be putting little square boxes on the ground and trees in various places. He had crept down under cover of darkness and investigated one of the boxes which he had come across. It didn't interest him much and, in fact, he had managed to knock it off its attachment while pushing it around. The men had returned again and had gone to where the boxes had been placed. He could watch them from his high vantage point without anyone even knowing he was there.

From that day on things became very different; people wandered around on a daily basis covering places where he did not often see anybody. He was having to be much more aware of being hidden, and using whatever cover he could. Finding anything to eat now was harder than ever. He even had to be careful at night, men with powerful torches wandered about and he had seen that some of the night time hunters carried guns. He was positive they were looking for him, he had seen men with guns before but they had killed the odd fox and many a rabbit at night. These particular men did not fire their guns at anything that he was aware of. He knew they were looking for him. He was absolutely sure about that. He felt like he had never felt before that his days as an escapee and fugitive were numbered.

The author's home at time of writing

COUNTDOWN

Spring was approaching. He could smell it in the air and in the soil; smells that as a prisoner he had not even thought about, or even been aware of. The days were getting longer and there were hundreds of lambs out on the pastures with their mothers. The sheep tended to be in the large fields nearer the village which were much more exposed and where the previous winter he would have taken a chance at night and taken the odd sickly lamb or even taken a lamb while the ewe was distracted by the labour pains of giving birth to a twin. Often, she did not seem to notice that the first one had gone, so busy was she cleaning up the second. He was much more wary now and had to admit to himself that his confidence had taken a severe bashing.

He moped around for what seemed like weeks. He felt weaker than he had done for a long time; he had not eaten a square meal for an age, everything was becoming a chore. He couldn't rest during the hours of day or night; he was always tense and on edge. he would set out full of enthusiasm for the next possible meal as he descended the hill but the slightest sound from any of the little farms be it human, dog or vehicle would send him streaming back up the hill often into the shelter of the dank cave systems. He felt the loss of bodyweight and with it his strength; no longer was he lithe, muscled and fit - he was now simply thin and weak.

He had been like this when he had first escaped but had soon adapted to his new found freedom; he had not got the choice of leaving the area totally as many escaped prisoners would and have done and had quickly in the early days found that regardless of the direction he took he eventually found himself cut off by the sea. Instead, he had to learn to keep himself out of sight and sound.

The undergrowth surrounding the cave and hill was freshening up and becoming green again; the trees were all in bud with cascading catkins. It did in one way make it easier to get around unseen but in his weakened state it was also more difficult to get around. He grew increasingly tired, some days he had to make himself get out of the cave simply to have fresh water from the stream instead of the smelly stagnant water remaining in the cave from the rains of winter.

The weather improved but unfortunately the number of walkers and hikers increased as well, with noticeably more people walking in his immediate area. He now had to hunt at night so as not to be seen – he did not catch much, he found his prey, he stalked it but his reactions were by now so slow that he failed more often than he succeeded.

His condition was worsening; he had sores now on his elbows and buttocks from pressure when lying down on what was now a hard-cold floor in the cave. He lacked any body fat and muscle now for protection. The pain in his stomach from constant hunger was agonising but now instead of driving him on to hunt as it used to it now made him simply want to curl up in a ball, keep warm and sleep.

FREEDOM ENDS

Days and nights drifted into one; he had an increasing feeling of impending doom. His own death did not seem to be too far away, he felt he had lost all his fight and enthusiasm for life. Spring was well advanced now - the grass was growing, he could smell it in the air, birds were active and full of song above him in the branches, soil was being worked in the fields but still he lay in the damp, dank cave.

Going out for water now was a struggle; the stream was literally only 20 feet away but it sapped all his strength to go and drink. Early one morning he crept out of the cave. He could barely climb out now - the drop down to the entrance hole was no problem on the way in and more often than not he half fell down but climbing up was more of a strength sapping task.

He slouched down, lapping gratefully at the clear water, drinking in long gulps until suddenly the silence was broken by a scream which seemed to tear the air apart, combined with a frantic barking. He looked around him, his reactions too slow to make his escape straight away then he turned to the direction of the noise. An elderly lady was making a hasty retreat along the path dragging the still yelping small dog by its lead.

The little dog's feet barely touched the ground as she dragged it away. He paused to collect his thoughts, his only aim was to get back into the shelter of his cave and lie low, his thirst quenched at least for the time being. Hunger was now far at the back of his mind, his weakness and deteriorating health made him lethargic and unenthusiastic about hunting. He dropped down the hole and entered the cave mouth. Sounds became a dull hum as he slipped in and out of a fitful sleep. Birds, sheep, horses, and distant dogs all merged into one. Ben did not know how long this went on for - he felt his life was slowly but surely ebbing away, felt drained, empty, and flat and totally without his in-built inherited sense of self-preservation. He was beyond care, he almost wanted to die.

In his minds wanderings he thought he heard voices again. Perhaps he was dreaming, no one had found him before and lots of people walked on the path through the woods. He ignored it, he was now drifting in and out of consciousness, and the feeling was almost comforting and warming.

The voices seemed nearer but he was unable to react; his body did not want to move. They seemed to be getting closer to his cave entrance now and - unlike the screaming woman with her dog and the people who had chased him - these voices were quieter. One voice seemed very close and although he hadn't a clue what was being said it was very soothing and in his confused mind bought back distant memories of his days as a prisoner. He remained relaxed but growled quietly almost as an acceptance of his inevitable demise. Suddenly he felt a sharp stabbing pain in his thigh; he tried to lift his head to react but a strange feeling was overtaking his body, a surreal floating. He felt as if he was lifting out of his own useless heap of a body and ascending to a totally different plane. If this was dying then it was bearable.

THE CAPTURE

The voices were coming back again. He lay quietly listening almost subconsciously to his surroundings; he could no longer hear the birds and the animals around him but there were people about. He felt heavy and drowsy in a different way to when he simply felt sleepy, he felt totally different almost renewed but still unable to consciously move around or react. The voices in his head were quite clear and loud now and he felt as if he was coming back from somewhere far away.

"He's coming round now" said one voice, the soothing one he had been aware of earlier. "The drip is well secured now. We will keep him a little light for a few days to keep him quiet. He will be fine".

He drifted off again, he was warm, comfortable and the terrible nagging in his guts had become far more subdued. He certainly couldn't remember eating, he was confused but didn't particularly care.

He could not tell how long this went on for; the voices drifted in and out of his head, sometimes he felt a pressure on some part of his body but was unable to do much more than twitch the muscle as a reaction to a touch that had been alien to him now for he couldn't remember how long.

"I'm going to take the line out now, John. I think we are winning with him now. He is rehydrated and I'm sure he will sort himself out slowly now with a bit of good grub when he comes round"

"That's great, "said another voice "I really thought we were going to lose him"

"Well we nearly did; another twenty-four hours and he would have been a goner"

"Well at least the country has the proof now that they are around"

He suddenly felt a sharp prick in his leg; he tried to pull it away but it was being held securely by someone's strong grip. The pain went and things seemed clearer in his head now. He even managed to make a sound, not his usual ferocious sound but a pathetic mewing sound that started somewhere at the back of his throat but refused to come any further.

"Come on now, John. Get out; he may look quiet now but he won't be in a minute"

"OK. I'm coming. I will just take the hood off his eyes then we will have to be quiet"

A NEW FUTURE

He was immediately aware of the light around him even though his eyelids were shut. The smells were strange yet frighteningly familiar; he felt the need to stretch his limbs which acted as if they had been unused for ever.

It felt good to stretch himself exposing all his claws. A sound started again in his throat - this time the full force of his voice exploded in a roar that frightened even him with its strength and power. He had been unable to use his voice for so long apart from a few times that he had almost forgotten the fierceness of the sound.

"There you go. Sounds fine to me", said the voice.

He leapt up aware now that he was in the vicinity of humans and was exposed to their glare. He made to run, crashed, got up again and crashed again; there was a wire mesh wall in every direction.

"Let's get out and let him settle "said the voice and he now saw two people on the other side of the mesh making their way towards a door.

The realisation hit him, he knew what had happened; a whirl of thoughts went through his feline mind, the need to escape, the need to hide and somewhere further inside his head the need to eat. He felt better than he had done in weeks.

The people had gone and he cowered for a while in the corner furthest from where they had gone to taking a minute to check his surroundings.

He was in a small room with a covering of deep straw on the floor, and water in a container on the wall. He could smell a familiar smell and on investigation found that a huge chunk of raw meat had been placed under the straw. He dared not approach it as yet. He also smelt a far more overpowering smell which was strange yet familiar to him.

Hours passed. All was quiet; the people had not returned so he crept towards the meaty smell on the ground, grabbed the hunk of leg and withdrew into the corner with it. He ate greedily and a full, satisfied feeling came over him. He lay contented in the straw; the only movement was an occasional flicker of the end of his tail. He started to clean himself, his fur smelt of the woods and he did not feel as sore as he had done.

He felt strangely happy.

Unbeknown to him he was being watched all the time; a camera placed high in his cage linked to another room meant the men could watch his every move.

Suddenly a door clanked. He leapt up and into the corner, ready to pounce. A metal door in one of the walls was sliding open. He backed away as it fell silent again. He sniffed; the air seemed fresh. He crept forward keeping low to the ground - on the attack - slowly he approached the door. Now he could see outside; there seemed to be an expanse of space, trees and a stream.

Maybe he was free again. Is that what he wanted? Cold, fear, hunger, persecution, loneliness? He wasn't sure any more.

He backed off and immediately his ears pricked again. What was that noise? He listened again; something was approaching the door; he made himself as small as he could. Was he going to be attacked? He waited.

Suddenly, a shadow was filling the doorway. He held his breath. Then standing just outside the doorway was a magnificent black leopard.

He did not know how to react; he now recognised the smell that he had been aware of earlier. The leopard growled and snarled at him; he was unsure how to react. He still cowered. She approached him steadily and confidently she got near enough to sniff him. He shrank into himself waiting for the attack and yet sensing that this was maybe not going to happen.

She came nearer and suddenly she was rubbing her head against him - her scent mingling with his. He relaxed and returned the gesture. She licked his mouth savouring the smell of the meat left on his breath. She moved away from him and looked back at him. He got to his feet and followed her; the air was suddenly sweet, the birds were singing, the trees were in full leaf – life, he felt, was going to be sweet.

(image actual photo of the 'beast' as captured by the author)

FACTS ON THE FICTION

This little book has been written by a woman who has had many personal sightings on her own land and local area of a big cat. Her theory is that the only way it could be there is that of a captive wild cat having been released and adapted itself to living wild. It has not harmed anyone. Only time will tell on that score. But is it a happy Big Cat or is it totally miserable and lonely? No one will know that either. The locals have got used to it and a group of them openly discuss their sightings amongst themselves, but the rest of the population probably think they are "Away with the fairies"!!!! Let's hope that this Big Cat's story will have a happy ending.

Imprisonment for a captive bred wildcat is possibly the only way it can be safe from cowboys with guns and young lads with airguns and farmers protecting their living by laying bait and traps. The area this has been based on is the big cats chosen area. An ideal place if someone as suspected did indeed choose to release it. It is a village called Llanddona on the Island of Anglesey in North Wales.

A village which sprawls down a vast wooded hillside of semi abandoned fields and woodlands right down to a ten square mile beach. The hill above is forested and until more recently would rarely have been walked through. The lower slopes towards the beach, an area locally known as Wern Woods or more commonly Bluebell woods is overgrown with wild seeded and uncontrolled sycamore saplings, hiding a short network of caves which burrow along the hills. Many of the cave mouths long blocked up with bedsteads and tree roots.

The author's smallholding was at the centre of the length of beach and three times the Cat was seen by herself and on another occasion by another family member, only once at night, the other times in broad daylight .

During the few years of visitations there were some stock losses locally, a young bullock virtually disembowelled and almost totally eaten overnight on a farm nearer to Pentraeth, and a mare whose hindquarters had been torn and damaged by long claw marks. Two large foals also disappeared from the author's property, one never to be found at all, and the second after a day's search, a hindquarter was discovered in the undergrowth at the seaward side of a field. Far too much for an average fox to devour overnight. The foal would likely not have been taken down by a fox anyway being a few months old and quite large.

Years have passed now since these sightings between around 2000-2010, the cat would vary from being sleek and black in the summer and a slightly browner dull coated appearance through the winters.
It is well known that a few men with guns tried to track it down during this period but never succeeded. Whether it has died by now in 2020 is unknown and quite likely.

Interest was shown in its existence by a wildlife enthusiast from the local BBC Wales Radio centre in Bangor and he was responsible for putting up a number of specialists night time cameras around the vicinity of these sightings but sadly nothing significant was picked up.

It did not seem to fear humans though as far as we know it never chose to interact, never running away briskly but a pause for a look and then idly sauntering away.

The author based the story on not mentioning that Ben was an actual big cat until the end , He or she is thought to have been a Melanistic Puma, apparently a Black Panther crossed with a fawn coloured puma is the experts opinion who declared that if we indeed had evidence of an actual Black Panther in the locality , we would have had walkers and ramblers going missing.

Whatever its demise, the author hopes that it had a happy existence on its chosen patch in a beautiful area of Anglesey.

ABOUT THE AUTHOR

The author lives on the Island of Anglesey off North Wales, her interests are the outdoors and through the 2020 Covid lockdown a new found interest in DIY! She was previously a college lecturer and British Horse society Examiner, and now a First Aid Trainer. She has also been a Coastguard Volunteer for over twenty years enjoying all aspects of the job.

Her main love was her horse breeding business alongside her late husband Mike and business partner Jane Roberts. She has delivered a fair few evening lectures on their involvement with equine artificial insemination. She now spends her time, teaching and looking after her geriatric horses and rescue hens whilst dreaming of writing her first novel in the campervan. We can all dream

Printed in Great Britain
by Amazon